Halloween Echo

by Susan Clymer

Illustrated by Stella Ormai

SCHOLASTIC INC.

New York Toronto London Auckland Sydney

With love
to the best nieces in the world,
Diane Elizabeth Clymer
and
Catherine Jane Clymer,
two of my best critics.

ISBN 0-590-46164-8

12 11 10 9 8 7 6 5 4 3 2 1   3 4 5 6 7 8/9

Printed in the U.S.A.   40

First Scholastic printing, September 1993

1. The New Neighbor

Jennifer skipped down her front steps and along the sidewalk after Lisa on her way to school. Spaghetti and meatballs, she thought happily. She and Lisa were as close as spaghetti and meatballs. They had been best friends forever. As usual, Jennifer's little brother Joshua followed right behind her like a shadow.

"Look!" Jennifer stopped skipping and pointed at the giant oak tree next door. Way up high in the branches crouched a woman.

"That's your new neighbor?" Lisa asked.

The woman was crawling on her hands and knees along a thick branch, muttering. She sounded angry, but Jennifer couldn't understand a single word. What in the holey moley was a lady doing way up there?

"She's weird," Lisa whispered.

"Crazy. Crazy. Crazy," Joshua sang. He danced around the two girls in a circle.

If her little brother had been an ant, Jennifer would have squashed him. "Hush!"

Joshua stopped in the middle of a hop, and his face puckered as if he wanted to cry.

"Sorry, squirt." Jennifer ruffled his hair. "We just don't want the lady to know we're here." She leaned her schoolbooks against the old tree stump and stared over the top of the tall white fence. They hadn't had a stranger move onto their block in years. She wished Mr. O'Dell still lived next door. He had been her friend for as long as she had memories. Jennifer sighed. Before Mr. O'Dell had left, she had promised him to try to like the new neighbor.

She hadn't expected the neighbor to be like this.

The woman wore brown corduroy pants, a bright red-and-yellow-striped T-shirt, and a cap. She looked like a kid . . . or a baseball player.

"Whoever heard of an old lady in a tree?" Lisa asked.

Jennifer certainly couldn't imagine her Grandma climbing trees. She noticed the woman's bright red hair peeking out from under her cap. "She isn't old."

Lisa dropped her lunch box right over Jennifer's foot. "Ooops."

Jennifer gasped, dancing aside. Lisa must have done that *on purpose*. Lisa hated having people disagree with her. In her mind, Jennifer yelled, "You are a foot-squashing vampire!" But she didn't say it out loud.

Just then, the woman in the tree started making hissing noises as she crawled along.

Jennifer saw something move on the end of the limb, something furry. "Hey, there's a cat up there." Then she saw a long striped tail. "Mr. Davis's cat, Milks!" Mr. Davis lived behind them.

The strange woman hissed, then growled . . . louder and louder. She sounded like three cats in a fight, all by herself. The palms of Jennifer's hands prickled.

"A grown-up pretending she's a cat?" Lisa sounded disgusted, yet she grabbed Jennifer's arm.

"A mad cat," Joshua whispered.

Milks sat down on the narrowest part of the limb. The woman crawled closer and waved one arm. "Pet attacker! Stay away from my house!" she yelled. The cat began washing his head, safely out of her reach.

Jennifer gasped. Milks was known all over the neighborhood for his hunting

"crimes," as Dad liked to call them. Had Milks caught the poor lady's pet bird right after she'd moved in?

The woman sighed and sat back down on the branch. She pretended to lick the back of her hand and rub her hand along her head.

"Yuck!" Lisa spit out the word. "Now she's washing herself just like the cat."

Joshua leaned against Jennifer's stomach. "That's bonkers!" Bonkers was his new word for the week. He must have used it two million times since Saturday.

Jennifer stared, beginning to be intrigued. No one like this lady had ever lived on their block before. Probably no one this odd had ever lived in their whole town of Palomar. Maybe not in all of Missouri. And she had moved in right next door.

Lisa nudged Jennifer and pointed at Joshua. He had both his hands squished together under his chin the way he always did when he was frightened. Lisa began making scary music sounds to rile him even more. Joshua jiggled from foot to foot. Jennifer couldn't resist whispering soft ghost noises into his ear. "OooooooOOOoooo."

She looked back at the tree in time to see the cat lean over to bite at the fur on its front leg. Immediately, the woman stretched her head down as if to nibble her own arm.

Joshua exploded. "She *is* crazy!" He screeched so loudly that both girls hopped backward.

The woman jerked her head toward the sound. Jennifer ducked behind the stump. "Oh, Joshua," she muttered. "Now the lady knows we're here!" The woman wobbled on the branch.

"Let's go," Lisa ordered. "Before she sees us."

The woman began to slide sideways, frantically wrapping her arms around the fat tree limb.

"She's falling!!" Jennifer jumped onto the tree stump so she could see better. "We can't just leave!" Her little brother and Lisa had already begun to run.

With an awful groan, the woman lunged with her right hand and caught hold of a smaller limb. What if the branch broke? The woman was almost as far off the ground as the top of a house. She screamed as the limb bent.

Jennifer pressed her thumbs over her ears and her fingers over her eyes. But not seeing was worse. She spread her fingers. The woman still hung from the small limb. She had a foot hooked over the big branch, and her other foot dangled. Her body looked like a giant Y in the air.

"The school bell. You'll be late!" Joshua shrieked, as if that were the most important thing in the whole world. Jennifer ignored him.

The woman slowly reached for another branch. She stretched and stretched her left arm. Jennifer could almost feel her own fingers curving around that branch as the lady grabbed. Then the lady swung her feet down to another limb. She was safe! Instantly, she twisted her head toward the tree stump.

Jennifer grabbed her books and ran.

2. Grow Up!

Panting, Jennifer slid into her seat as the second tardy bell stopped ringing. "Yippie skippie!" she muttered. "I'm not late!" Jennifer hoped Lisa had made it to her classroom in time, too. Lisa was only four months older, but she was in a higher grade.

Her teacher, Ms. Adams, cleared her throat, the way she always did when a student did something mildly wrong. "Good morning, class."

For the next hour, Jennifer tried to concentrate on multiplying with math manipulatives, but her mind kept seeing her strange new neighbor pretending to be a cat.

Six minutes before recess, Jennifer's best school friend, Betsy, leaned across her desk. "When are you going to get your dice?" Betsy whispered.

Jennifer stopped swinging her feet and looked around the classroom. The girls all wore little dice on chains. Not just four or five girls, like a couple of days ago, but everyone had a pair . . . everyone except her. They wore the tiny chains hooked through the buttonholes on their sleeves or in their shoelaces. Holes had been drilled through the spots so the hard plastic dice could be hung on the chains. The girls wore all different colors—red, green, blue, even purple. Betsy's bright orange pair dangled from the clasp on her overalls.

Since Betsy was her friend, Jennifer told her the truth. "I guess I don't like dice that much." Then Jennifer giggled. "Hey,

I could wear Silly Willy on a chain tomorrow. Or you could," she added generously. Silly Willy was Jennifer's tiny stuffed lion that Betsy had liked when she had come over after school.

The next time the teacher wasn't looking, Betsy leaned over and whispered to Shannon, the most popular girl in the class. Then, on the playground, Shannon announced in her best singsong voice, "Jennifer doesn't like our *silly* fad."

No one listened when Jennifer tried to explain that she'd been talking about her lion named Silly, not the dice.

After recess, Jennifer dreamed up a million revenges. She wanted to dip Shannon's hairbrush in green dye during gym class so that when Shannon used the brush her hair would turn lime-green. She wished she could shrink Betsy to the size of the dice. Jennifer imagined dripping glue on all the girls' chairs so that they would stick forever.

When Jennifer finally ran out of revenges, she started thinking about her strange neighbor again. Jennifer decided she would think of her as the Catlady. She also decided that she wanted to talk to Dad . . . *alone*. He would know if the lady was really crazy as Joshua thought.

Jennifer doodled a cat in her journal. She and Lisa always walked home together. She would have to sneak away after school to avoid Lisa so that she could have a private talk with Dad.

At the end of the afternoon, Jennifer hurried out of the classroom and down the hall. She was the very first person outside. Jennifer ran down the fenced-in path through the middle of the wheat field.

Jennifer turned right at the first street and skipped past the new neighbor's house. If the Catlady looked out her window she wouldn't think Jennifer looked nervous. Kids always skipped. Right? She hoped the lady hadn't seen her clearly enough this morning to recognize her.

"Dad! Dad!" Jennifer hurried into their big three-story white house. Dad was always the one home after school in their home. He taught at the college in the mornings. Everyone in town called him the Professor. Mom worked at the Toy Shoppe until after five. Right now, Mom was gone. She went away for a month every fall to paint pictures. The rest of the family had gotten good at managing alone for a month.

"Guess what?" Jennifer exclaimed. Her father sat in the kitchen reading a magazine. He had sawdust all over himself, even in his hair and beard. He must have been sanding the new bookshelf in his basement workshop again.

"Guess what happened today?" she repeated.

Her father looked up at her. "Where's your brother?"

"Joshua?" Jennifer stopped jiggling.

Her father sighed. "Do you have another brother?"

"I . . . I forgot him," Jennifer admitted. Now that Joshua was in the first grade, she was supposed to walk home from school with him every day.

"You forgot your brother?" Her father closed the magazine. "Jennifer."

"Dad, something exciting happened this morning," Jennifer began. "I want to tell you—"

Her father headed for the basement. "Go find Joshua."

"Please, Dad! He's big enough to get home by himself."

Her father loved to hear how big Joshua was getting. It worked every time. He sat down in the chair nearest the basement door. "All right. Tell me. But hurry."

Jennifer told him about this morning, right from the beginning. Her father pulled on his beard, the way he always did when he was interested. He laughed once. Jennifer liked making Dad laugh. "And then the lady slipped, Dad. Joshua and Lisa ran off."

Her father regarded her with a frown that made his eyebrows bunch up. Jennifer hopped onto their tall kitchen ladder and pretended to act out the lady's part in the tree. Acting would make this even better. She couldn't resist getting carried away. "The lady fell and crashed onto another branch."

Jennifer jumped off the ladder and tapped herself on the chest. "I watched from the old stump."

Then she stepped back onto the ladder. "The lady grabbed the branch, and it started to break!" Jennifer hung from the rounded top of the ladder and imitated the woman's voice. "Help me! Help me!"

Her father sighed and looked down at the floor.

Jennifer jumped off the ladder again to act out her own part. "*I* climbed over the fence." She pantomimed reaching for the top and swinging her leg over.

"Jennifer, that fence is six feet high," her father interrupted.

She was too excited to stop. "I got over in five seconds I was so scared." Jennifer ran around and around the ladder. "Then I held my arms up. 'I'll catch you, lady,' I cried.

"Dad, the lady caught herself on the third branch that she hit. If she had gone through one more, she would have squashed me. Squashed!"

"Jennifer." Something in her father's tone of voice stopped her. Jennifer looked over at him. Her father was standing, one hand on the basement door. "When are you going to stop making up stories?" he asked.

Jennifer blushed and dropped her arms. She had added a bit. "Most of it is true, Dad."

Her father wasn't listening. "Jennifer, grow up!" He thumped down the basement stairs. "And go find your brother."

Go find your brother. That's all anybody ever cared about—Joshua. Jennifer stared at the door going down into the basement. She hadn't even started telling Dad about the important stuff, about how she felt about the lady.

When Jennifer opened the door to the back porch, she heard her little brother singing, "Grow up. Grow up."

Joshua had heard! Jennifer slammed the door and ran up the steps into her bedroom. She threw herself down on the bed and covered her burning ears so she couldn't hear her brother's chant. He must have been mad that she'd deserted him after school. Now he'd heard Dad. She would have to think of a way to keep him from telling Lisa. Then Jennifer had a horrible thought. What if Joshua repeated her story to all the kids at school! One of his friends had a sister in her class.

If Joshua were smaller, Jennifer knew she could sit on him and not let him go until he promised never to tell. He wasn't that small anymore. Suddenly Jennifer thought of another way to be sure he'd keep quiet.

Jennifer sneaked out of her room and quietly opened the door to Joshua's room. Right on his dresser sat his starship model. His favorite teddy bear leaned against his pillow. She took them both. Later she would warn Joshua to keep quiet, so he could have his toys back again.

Jennifer hid the teddy bear in the back of the closet with the towels. Then she put the starship in her underwear drawer. He wouldn't dare look there.

Jennifer sat down on her bed so hard that it squeaked. She hadn't added *that* much when she'd told Dad about the Catlady. Jennifer hugged her old stuffed kangaroo and Silly Willy against her chest. Was making up stories really a little kid's thing to do?

She could almost hear the scorn in her friends' voices from earlier that day at school. Even Betsy had treated her like a baby, just because she didn't want to wear the dice. Jennifer shivered.

Did everyone think she was just a little kid? Did she really need to grow up?

3. The Bike Race

Jennifer shuffled home from school through the red and yellow leaves on the sidewalk. She loved the crisp, crackling sounds of fall. Beside her, Lisa tossed acorns at trees. Joshua scurried ahead and then circled back through the deepest leaves, making train noises, "Whoo! Whoo!"

All weekend, the three of them had played on Jennifer and Joshua's front porch, waiting for the Catlady to appear. After Monopoly and Crazy Eights, Jennifer had made up an acting game. The three children had pretended that the neighbor lady worked as a zookeeper who imitated the animals.

They hadn't seen their new neighbor

once since that day in the tree.

Jennifer kicked some leaves as high as her head. Too bad she couldn't have missed seeing *Shannon* lately. Shannon and some other girls in her class had stared at her all day as if she had mustard on her nose, or something.

Lisa sat on Jennifer's front steps. "Let's ride bikes."

"Wow, bikes!" Joshua raced toward the backyard as fast as his legs would take him.

"How about building card houses on the porch?" Jennifer suggested.

Lisa pointed to the treetops. "Too windy."

Jennifer shrugged. Lisa was probably right.

Lisa held up four fingers in their signal for "See you in four minutes." She dashed halfway down the block toward home before Jennifer even got in her front door.

Jennifer dropped her books on the

table. "We're home, Dad." She headed upstairs to her bedroom and pulled on her jeans, listening to Joshua sputter outside like a motorcycle. She'd already given back his teddy bear so he could sleep. She had promised to return his starship when he had kept silent for a week about the story she'd told Dad.

On her way downstairs, Jennifer jumped onto her right foot and tapped her left heel to her toes. Then she hopped onto her left foot and tapped her toes. The secret stair step shuffle, she called it.

Lisa threw open the front door with a crash. "Who is living under your stairs this week?"

"A tap-dancer," Jennifer replied. "She's waiting to discover kids and whisk them away to dance in the movies."

Lisa joined her on the steps, tap-dancing loudly.

She and Lisa had played this game for

years. One summer Jennifer had created a Wild Girl under the stairs who would lead them on adventures. She and Lisa had gotten into awful trouble, particularly the time they had dragged the kitchen ladder onto the balcony, then climbed onto the roof. Dad had called the fire department to save them.

"Pipe down up there!" Dad yelled from the basement. "What are you doing, bouncing lead basketballs?"

"Hello, Professor!" Lisa called. She tap-danced out the front door.

Jennifer headed through the kitchen to grab four of the cookies Mom had made before she left on her painting trip. She joined Joshua and Lisa. They rested on their bikes in front of the neighbor's house. Jennifer handed out the cookies and gave Joshua two. It made him miss Mom less.

"Your neighbor climbs trees and acts

weird," Lisa said with her mouth full. "What else do you think she does?"

"She waves her hands when she walks," Joshua said.

Jennifer turned toward him. "How do you know?" Then she realized that Lisa had said exactly the same words. Jennifer balanced on her bike seat and leaned forward to tap her forehead against her friend's. They always did that when they spoke in unison.

Joshua pedaled madly away up the sidewalk.

"Joshua!" Lisa yelled.

"I saw her in her house," he said over his shoulder.

Lisa raced her bike in front of his and squealed to a stop. "What do you mean?" Joshua bumped into her. Lisa nodded to Jennifer to take the back wheel. "All right, kid. Tell us everything," Lisa commanded.

Jennifer pulled in behind him, though

she could see from her little brother's face that he wasn't sure whether to smile or cry. He turned his head back and forth between the two of them, and his lip quivered. Jennifer thought, Maybe I should give him back his starship tonight.

"I . . . I went up in the attic," Joshua stuttered. "There's a little window. I could see."

Jennifer's mouth fell open. "You watched her?" she demanded. "You stared into someone else's house?"

Lisa hit him on the shoulder lightly with her fist. "Good boy!" Joshua grinned.

"No, he's not!" Jennifer exclaimed.

Joshua bounced on his bicycle seat. "The lady walked all around and waved her arms. No one else was there!"

"Now we'll really get to see what she's like." Lisa stared over Joshua's head at Jennifer. "Invite me to dinner and to spend the night. We'll watch her."

Lisa acted so bossy sometimes. If you didn't agree with her, she would push you around like a hippopotamus.

"Friday night," Lisa said. "Four days from now."

On the other hand, Jennifer had to admit she'd been dying to see the lady again. It was as if someone had read her the first chapter of a mystery and then run off with the book.

"Jennifer?" Lisa asked in a cold voice.

Jennifer twisted the foam pads on her handlebars. She swallowed past a sudden lump of worry in her throat. She and Lisa were still best friends, like spaghetti and meatballs . . . right?

Finally, she nodded. "Okay. Friday night."

With a Comanche yell, Lisa zipped out into the street. "Let's ride to Hetmer

Hill!" Joshua followed, yelling louder. He couldn't ride on the street except with the big kids.

Jennifer didn't move. Dad would be furious at them for looking into someone else's house. Furious! He would roast Joshua and her and serve them at the university luncheon. Actually, he would call Mom. Jennifer knew she would have to explain over and over until Mom understood every detail. Jennifer shivered. Why had she agreed to spy?

Because she couldn't resist, that's why.

Lisa and Joshua disappeared around the corner. "Wait!" Jennifer cried and pedaled to catch up. Jennifer barreled around the corner without stopping at the sign. Right in her path, someone rested sideways on a bicycle. Jennifer stood on her brakes as hard as she could. The rider looked familiar. Jennifer stopped, only an inch from the woman's bike.

"You're lucky." The woman's voice cracked. "You're lucky I wasn't a car." Her red hair was pulled back in a ponytail. She had the brightest green eyes Jennifer had ever seen.

Jennifer stared up at her, speechless. This was the neighbor who climbed trees. This was the weird lady who pretended she was a cat. Worst of all, this was the person she had just agreed to spy on.

The woman sighed. "Then again, *I'm* lucky you stopped."

She must not have recognized them! Jennifer swallowed, relieved. Lisa and Joshua rested on their bikes only a few feet away.

"Cat got your tongue?" the woman asked, smiling.

Jennifer and Lisa looked at each other.

"I know I talk to myself," the small slender woman said. "But not usually when I'm standing so close to someone."

Jennifer eased her bike back a step while Lisa moved one finger in tiny circles by the side of her head. Joshua exploded into a laugh, then changed the sound to a sneeze.

"Want to race?" the woman asked. "Since you don't seem to talk. Clearly you like to ride fast, and I'd enjoy some exercise."

Jennifer's tongue stuck to the roof of her mouth as if she'd eaten a spoonful of peanut butter. She shook her head.

"I'll race!" Lisa said.

"Me, too," Joshua cried.

"Funny . . . I recognize that voice," the woman said.

Joshua blushed. He *had* been the one whose yell had made her fall.

Joshua rolled his bike closer to Jennifer, and she reached for his hand. The woman stared at each of their faces. When it was Jennifer's turn, she could swear she felt the lady's gaze in her mind like a rush of wind.

"Nice of you all to ask," the woman finally said. "I didn't hurt myself when I slipped." Her voice rose to a higher pitch. "But I was upset all day. Thank your lucky dragon's foot, I didn't see you then."

None of the children moved. Joshua turned redder.

The woman rolled her bike forward. "Come on. Come on. It's over now, and I'm not going to bite. Let's line up."

Jennifer followed as if in a haze.

"To the top of Hetmer Hill." The woman pointed one long finger at Joshua. "You call it. By the way, my name's Echo."

"Ready," Joshua piped. His voice shook. "Go!"

At first, they all rode next to each other. Then Joshua fell behind. Partway up the hill, Jennifer began to lose ground. She pedaled so hard that hot pains ran up her calves. Lisa and the lady were riding neck and neck.

Echo? What an odd name. Now that the lady wasn't right next to her, Jennifer felt as if . . . as if she'd been released from some power. She'd never heard of a grown-up who raced a bicycle. And what did Echo mean by "lucky dragon's foot"? Maybe she carried a fake dragon's foot for good luck instead of a rabbit's? Three-fourths of the way up the hill, Lisa and Echo still biked side by side. Then Lisa started to fall behind.

Jennifer had never won a race against Lisa, not even once. A little part inside of Jennifer cheered. Echo was ahead of Lisa by two lengths when she rolled over the top.

Jennifer caught up, panting. "What a race!" she exclaimed. Lisa glared and dumped her bike. She even stomped around. But Echo had a smile on her face.

So did Joshua when he finally caught up. Jennifer grinned, though she tried not to let her friend see. "My name is Jennifer," she said to Echo.

The weird neighbor lady had beaten Lisa!

4. Spying

Jennifer fished deep into her pocket. "Promise you won't tell?" she whispered to Betsy. Jennifer glanced around the room to make sure no one was watching. The class was working in pairs on their animal projects. Betsy stopped coloring the frog legs on their picture. She nodded, curious. Jennifer pulled her Parcheesi dice out of her pocket and laid them on her friend's desk. "See? I've got my dice."

Betsy covered her mouth with one hand to stifle a giggle.

Jennifer's shoulders tensed, but she flicked over a Parcheesi die as if she were perfectly calm. "What's wrong? Dad could help me drill the holes in these so I could hang—"

"Those dice are old!" Betsy exclaimed softly.

Old dice weren't any good? Jennifer couldn't bear being embarrassed again. She thought as fast as she could. "Of course, they're old." Jennifer's voice dropped to her best whisper. "Old dice are better." She'd read something once in a novel about Gypsies that might help her. "You don't think dice are only for games, do you?"

Betsy leaned closer. Their shoulders touched.

"Dice were once thought to be very *powerful* for fortune-telling and good-luck charms," Jennifer murmured. "The older the dice the better." She picked up a pencil to label the parts of their frog. "Ms. Adams is watching us."

Minutes later, Jennifer shoved the dice firmly into her pocket as she and Betsy hurried to gym class. That had been close!

The troublesome Parcheesi dice would go back in the game tonight, and stay there!

Today was Friday, so tonight Lisa would be coming over to spy. Jennifer wished the evening could be here *now*. The rest of her day at school crept past with the speed of a turtle.

At dinner, every bite seemed to take forever. Dad was in one of his great moods. That made Jennifer nervous. She hadn't done anything in ages that she knew her parents would disapprove of this much.

Finally, Jennifer knelt beside Lisa, their elbows resting on the attic windowsill. They had told Dad they wanted to play a game of hide-and-seek in the attic. No adults allowed. He had agreed to send Joshua up after he got him ready for bed.

From the attic window, Jennifer could see into Echo's brightly lit kitchen. The room looked *normal* with a table, chairs, and a giant plant as big as a tree. How

disappointing! The upstairs room wasn't so well lit. Jennifer could make out a computer on a table with papers strewn everywhere. Something jabbed her in the ribs. "Stop poking me!"

"I'm not!" Lisa muttered.

Jennifer stared straight out the window. She wanted to be the first to catch sight of Echo. Ever since the bicycle race, she had wanted to see her again. Sometimes, telling someone your name was the first step to being friends.

An elbow shoved at Jennifer again. Still without looking, she reached over to pinch Lisa. A blond head popped up between them. "Joshua," Jennifer sighed. He was in his pajamas, the teddy bear under one arm.

"I'm sneaking," Joshua said. "Look! She's there."

Jennifer turned her head to see. She had only taken her eyes off the window for two seconds because of Joshua, and *he* had been the one to see her first.

Echo walked slowly onto her second-floor balcony, like a queen. She wore a long black robe and carried a candle in her hand.

"Turn out the light," Lisa demanded. "So Echo can't see us."

Jennifer almost said, "You do it." But Lisa was the guest tonight. Outside, the lady set the candle down on the balcony railing. This was almost like watching a movie. Jennifer ran to the center post, flipped off the light, and ran back. Echo had her arms raised in the air. She was making an odd noise that Jennifer could barely hear.

"She's barking," Joshua piped cheerfully. "She's barking at the dragon she keeps in her basement. She said she has lucky dragon feet, remember?"

Lisa ruffled his hair. "Why would she be *barking* at a dragon, squirt?"

The Catlady leaned over and blew out the candle. Slowly she lifted her arms and twirled in a circle. Then she began to sing, an odd song where the notes slid into each other. Jennifer felt worry creeping into her head like a spider. Perhaps she shouldn't have told Echo her name.

"Do dragons eat boys?" Joshua whispered.

"Not usually," Lisa replied, enjoying herself.

"Maybe she's practicing for Halloween," Jennifer said. "It's only three weeks away." Jennifer suddenly missed her old neighbor so much. Every Halloween, Mr. O'Dell had put a barrel of apples and soft sand on his front porch. Everybody who came got to bob for an apple if they wanted. The trick was to get an apple without a mouthful of sand.

Echo stretched her arms out in front of her as if she were calling someone.

"Over there!" Lisa pointed. The moon rose above the trees in the neighbor's yard. "She's singing to the moon?"

Joshua stiffened.

"She couldn't be!" Shivery chills crept down Jennifer's back. What if Echo *were* someone terrible? Then Jennifer remembered how she had felt during the bicycle race, as if she were coming out from under a spell. What if Echo were a . . .

"She's . . . she's a witch!" Joshua raised his fist to pound on the window. "Go away, WITCH!" Joshua started wailing like a three-year-old. Lisa clamped one hand over his mouth. Now Joshua sounded like a siren.

Jennifer grabbed his fist. She didn't want Dad coming up here. "She might turn you into a bat-troll if she hears you," she whispered. Being turned into a bat-troll used to be her little brother's greatest nightmare. Mom and Dad had never been able to figure out exactly what a bat-troll was.

Joshua stopped howling right in the middle of a wail.

"Witches aren't real," Jennifer insisted. Still, Joshua had said what she'd been wondering herself and that made her feel uneasy. When Lisa released him, Joshua leaned up against her, clutching his teddy bear in his arms.

The lady bent over and waved her palms over the floor of the balcony. "She's calling up spirits!" Lisa exclaimed.

"She must be practicing for Halloween," Jennifer repeated stubbornly, for Joshua's sake. Her voice shook. Jennifer wanted to dash downstairs and hide her face in her father's stomach just as if she were the one who was six years old. Echo went back inside.

A moment later, Echo stuck her head out the balcony door. She peered around as if she were looking for someone. Then she tiptoed across the balcony. She had taken off the robe and was wearing a sweat suit. Echo crouched down behind her lawn chair. Then she stared up at the place where she had been standing earlier.

"She's pretending to be someone else," Jennifer murmured. "Actually, she looks as if she's watching who she was a minute ago . . . when she was wearing the robe."

"What if she has two people inside of her?" Lisa's voice squeaked higher. "I saw this movie once about a woman who had two people inside of her." Then Lisa gasped. "One part of the woman was a nice doctor and the other one robbed houses!"

"A robber?" Jennifer cried.

Lisa slammed her hands down on the windowsill so hard that Joshua stumbled backward and fell. He landed on the seat of his pants, but he didn't cry.

"We have to keep track of that lady," Lisa said fiercely. "We have to *watch* her."

5. Snapping Dragons and Nipping Cats

Jennifer and Lisa and Joshua spent their free time for a week spying in the attic. They carried up picnics of pickles and cold chicken and cheese. They sang songs and acted out more Catlady scenes.

Today Lisa hadn't been able to come over after school. So Jennifer sat in her stairwell, talking to the grandmotherly woman who lived under her stairs this week. She was telling her about what had happened at school today.

During recess, Shannon had teased Jennifer about old dice being used for fortune-telling. Half the class had heard. Shannon had put one hand on her hip and said sweetly, "Some people can't help making up stories, you know."

Jennifer had been so shocked that she had blurted out, "I didn't make that one up. Someone else did."

And everyone had *laughed*.

Jennifer imagined the old grandmotherly woman suggesting that she "just stand up and dance Shannon's meanness right out of her mind." So Jennifer danced the secret stair step shuffle as hard as she could. Then she skipped into the kitchen to get herself a sandwich.

"Well, Jack-in-the-box," Dad said fondly, looking up from his toolbox. "What are you going to be for Halloween?"

Jennifer pulled the peanut butter off the shelf. "A big cat."

"There sure has been a lot of talk about cats around here," Dad mused. He started counting on his fingers. "You're reading *Ten Tales About Cats*. Joshua is reading *The Cat in the Hat*. Actually, I'm reading it to him." He held up a third finger. "You keep telling us cat superstitions. My favorite was the one you told at dinner last night, 'A girl who wants to be married should feed a cat from her old shoes.' " Dad lifted a fourth finger. "You're in the attic a lot. You're not hiding a cat up there, are you?" he teased.

Jennifer yanked the salami out of the

refrigerator and slammed the door. "Absolutely, fabsolutely *not.*" Just to be safe, she changed the subject. "What do *you* want to be for Halloween, Dad?" Her father always dressed up and tried to scare the children who came to the door. It was a Halloween tradition in their town. Even the college kids came to see the Professor in his costume.

"Death," Dad answered in an eerie voice. Joshua came into the kitchen, and Dad leaned over him with his arms wide.

"Daddy?" Joshua looked up at him. His voice cracked.

"Dad's talking about his Halloween costume," Jennifer explained. She bit into her sandwich. She adored peanut butter and salami.

"I'm going to be a dragon," Joshua announced. "Can you help me?"

"Help you?" Dad swooped up Joshua in his arms. "I was hoping you'd ask. Do you want to be a snarling dragon or a friendly one?" He carried Joshua downstairs to look through their trunk of costumes.

Jennifer zipped back up two flights of stairs to the attic with her snack. This was a great chance to do a little spying. Something was bound to happen sooner or later. She and Joshua and Lisa hadn't seen Echo do anything other than write in a notebook or read a book all week.

Just as Jennifer reached the attic window, Echo stepped out her kitchen door. She was carrying a bag and a shovel.

Echo crossed her yard and started digging. She took mysterious things out of her bag and planted them.

Jennifer didn't feel bad about spying, not anymore. She had decided that she needed to know *everything* about the crazy, witchy Catlady.

Echo's garden had hundreds of flowers in all different colors. Some of the flowers, like those dark red mums in the corner, had been planted by Mr. O'Dell. Echo finished her gardening and wandered toward the fence.

Jennifer gripped the windowsill. Hey, all of Mom's plants had died at that early frost. Jennifer's heart beat faster. Come to think of it, Echo had the only yard on the block with lots of flowers still alive. How had she done it?

Echo picked a batch of yellow blossoms. Then she stood in front of the patch with her arms crossed and talked. She was talking to the flowers! Is that how Echo kept the flowers alive? Jennifer imagined the flowers nodding their heads back. This was the battiest thing the Catlady had done yet. Yet Jennifer had to admit, it would be kind of fun if plants *could* talk.

* * *

The next morning, Jennifer hurried down her front steps in a rainstorm to meet Lisa. "Guess who I saw yesterday?"

"It's raining cats and dogs!" Joshua yelled, repeating what Jennifer had said at breakfast. Then he leaped for a puddle. Muddy water splashed over both girls. They screamed as Joshua raced up the sidewalk.

One moment, Jennifer saw her brother's mouth fall open. The next moment, Echo rushed out of her gate, and Joshua crashed into her. Echo helped Joshua regain his footing. She looked confused, as if she hadn't expected to see anyone. "Sorry," she said. "I was . . . thinking."

Joshua scurried away.

Echo's dazed eyes focused on Jennifer. She touched her on the shoulder with one finger. "Dream!" she commanded cheerfully. Then Echo gave a little wave and hurried away. Jennifer couldn't take her eyes off her.

"Wombat," Joshua whispered. That was his new word for the week.

Echo glided down the street, skirting puddles. She didn't carry an umbrella or even wear a hat.

"Look at her feet!" Lisa exclaimed. Echo wore one green sock and one yellow. Jennifer had never seen anyone who wore two different-colored socks. Lisa muttered, "She does that because she has two people inside of her."

Together the children watched Echo disappear. Jennifer realized she was holding her breath. "Dream," Echo had said. Did she mean go to sleep and dream? Or daydream, like Jennifer sometimes dreamed about being an astronaut?

A raindrop trickled down Jennifer's neck. Then another. That woke her up. "I saw Echo yesterday. She was talking to flowers!" Jennifer told Lisa the whole story. "Who ever heard of planting in October?" Then she added, "I figured out Echo must have been planting catnip."

Water dripped off the brim of Lisa's rain hat. "Since she's the Catlady, she might need catnip to roll in, right?"

Jennifer nodded, pleased that Lisa had gotten her joke.

"I think she rolls with her dragon," Joshua interrupted.

Lisa glared at him. She still had mud all over her jacket.

Jennifer snapped her fingers. "What about those flowers called snap*dragons*? Echo could have been planting some snapdragons!" Jennifer narrowed her eyes at Joshua. "They could all come alive." She stepped toward her little brother. "Snapping dragons!"

Joshua backed away, startled. Jennifer

stalked after him, and Joshua began running. Jennifer gave Lisa a "come on!" signal and followed him. This would teach Joshua.

"The catnip, too. Hundreds of nipping cats!" Lisa joined the chase, pretending to nip Joshua with her hands. "All coming alive on Halloween."

Joshua screamed. He waved his arms while he ran. They chased him through the wheat field right into the school.

Lisa leaned against Jennifer, giggling. Jennifer squeezed Lisa's hand. She laughed so hard her stomach hurt. How could she have ever doubted that she and Lisa would be best friends forever?

6. She's Dangerous!

Two weeks after they'd seen Echo singing to the moon, Jennifer tiptoed down the attic stairs. Thank goodness, Dad was sleeping in as he usually did on Saturdays. Jennifer didn't want him knowing she'd been in the attic again. She and Lisa and Joshua had started taking turns spying so Dad wouldn't get any more suspicious.

Last week, Lisa had spotted the Catlady sitting on the top of her roof. There hadn't been a ladder anywhere! Joshua had been the luckiest. He had heard her howling like a wolf. Another time, he'd seen Echo sitting in a circle with four people. They had been holding hands.

Now it was her turn. Jennifer rubbed

her hands together. She finally had a good story to tell. She'd just seen Echo pretending to sword fight with an umbrella.

"Joshua? Ready to go meet Lisa?" Jennifer called at his door.

"I can't find my shoe," he wailed.

Jennifer sat down and slumped against the attic door to wait. Having a little brother was like having a pet tadpole. You never knew when he would change and grow up. Then again, if Joshua really were a tadpole, he would grow up into a frog. Jennifer imagined a frog with Joshua's face. "Hurry up!" She drummed her heels against the floor.

Jennifer pulled up her cuffs for about the tenth time to look at her socks. As an experiment, she had put on one blue sock and one red sock this morning. She thought it might make her feel strange, like Echo. Maybe even crazy.

It hadn't so far. To her surprise, Jennifer rather liked the brightness. Echo might be crazy, but she hadn't given them any real proof that she had two people inside of her . . . or even that she was mean, like Shannon.

Jennifer closed her eyes when she thought of Shannon. She had wondered a million times why she hadn't just given in and bought herself a pair of dice on a chain for school. Then her problem never would have gotten so bad.

A few days ago, two girls had started wearing thin plastic colored bracelets. Shannon had worn them on Friday. Probably most of the girls would be wearing them soon. Jennifer sighed. She did like the colors. Maybe she should go to the store this weekend.

Joshua bounded out of his bedroom.

"Ribbit. Ribbit." Jennifer imitated a frog. She made herself laugh, and laughing made her forget all about school.

Bicycling up to Hetmer Hill, Jennifer left Joshua way behind. She didn't want him to catch her going into the hideout, where she had arranged to meet Lisa.

For years, she and Lisa had kept their

hideout a secret. Hetmer Park had the biggest trees around. One of them had thick branches that came down all the way to the ground so no one could see inside—a perfect hideout. Jennifer loved it. This was the place where she and Lisa had first made up their game of tapping foreheads when they said something in unison.

Jennifer crawled under the branches of the pine tree just as Joshua reached the top of the hill.

He parked his bike next to hers. "Jennifer!"

She crawled faster. As she expected, Lisa was already in the hideout.

"Jennifer!" Joshua ran right past the tree toward the playground. All Jennifer saw were his feet. "I'll tell Dad!" he yelled, his voice fading as he moved away from the tree.

Lisa pointed to the bikes. By the time Joshua came back around the swing set, the two girls were sitting beside the bikes.

"Where were you? How did you get here?" Joshua demanded, panting.

"Magic," Lisa answered.

Joshua lay down on his belly in the grass. "Awww."

"Who has something to report?" Lisa asked. Jennifer wanted to save hers for last.

"Me!" Joshua raised his hand as if he were in school. "I saw a lady give Echo a backrub yesterday!"

Lisa stared at her palm. "So what? I followed her in the grocery store."

"You got that close?" Jennifer asked.

"When she saw me, I pretended I was with another lady," Lisa said. "I held onto her cart. I even waved at Echo."

Joshua looked at Lisa as if he thought

she were the bravest person in the whole world. "Did she steal anything?"

Jennifer rolled her eyes. Joshua was convinced that Echo was a robber.

"She bought weird stuff," Lisa answered. "Something called tofu that looks like a big white mud cake. It jiggles like Jell-O when you shake it. And mushrooms."

"Yuck!" Jennifer hated mushrooms.

"And have you ever heard of an adult drinking milk?"

"Mom drinks milk," Joshua said.

Jennifer poked him to make him shut up. She didn't want Lisa thinking their mom was weird, too.

"Is that it?" Lisa said.

Jennifer took a deep breath. "I saw her this morning in her attic." She had to make this good. "Echo waved an umbrella in her hand, like a sword." Jennifer jumped to her feet and acted out an imaginary sword fight. She wanted to do it as well as Echo had. Joshua laughed and clapped his hands. That was all that had really happened.

Lisa didn't seem impressed.

So Jennifer made up some more. "Echo had this old dress dummy set up. You know, the kind you see in stores?" Jennifer pointed at a little tree to show that it was the dummy. "Then Echo ran at the dummy screaming, 'I'll get you! I'll get you!' She yelled so loud that I could *hear* her."

Out of the corner of her eye, Jennifer saw Lisa watching now. "Echo knocked the dummy down. Then she stabbed the umbrella into the dummy's chest. Sawdust spurted everywhere!" Lisa's eyes widened, so Jennifer added one final bit. "Echo wiped off the tip of the umbrella on her pants and raised her hands in the air. Then she laughed!"

Joshua gasped.

"I couldn't watch anymore! I ran down our attic stairs and slammed the door," Jennifer exclaimed. "I'll tell you, I'm never going back up there to spy. The Catlady is—"

"Dangerous," Lisa finished the sentence, her voice icy.

"Dangerous," Joshua repeated, pulling an imaginary sword out of his belt.

"That's right! Mean and nasty." Jennifer flushed, completely carried away. "We've got to stop her, before she—"

Lisa leaped to her feet and slammed one fist into the palm of her other hand. "I *knew* she was dangerous! She talks to flowers. She howls like a dog sometimes." Lisa's voice rose to a cry. "She has two people inside of her, maybe more.

Now she pretended to stab somebody, and she laughed. That's evil! What if it was just practice for really stabbing somebody?"

Lisa's fierceness jolted Jennifer from her head to the bottom of her feet. The shock left her absolutely still.

"I knew she was dangerous!!" Lisa exclaimed.

Joshua swooshed his imaginary sword across the top of Jennifer's head. "Take that! And that!" Then he grabbed his chest as if he'd been stabbed. With a long curdling scream, he fell between the two girls.

"Be quiet!" Jennifer cried, so loudly that her voice cracked.

Suddenly it was as if Dad were in the back of Jennifer's mind, and they were standing in the kitchen together again, as they had been that first day she'd told him about Echo. He had his hand on the basement doorknob, and he was looking down at her.

In the middle of a scream, Joshua opened one eye. "I'm dead now," he whispered.

Jennifer leaned over Joshua and put her hand up on Lisa's arm. "That's not exactly what I meant . . . about Echo."

Lisa tightened her mouth. "She did stab that dummy, right?" Jennifer sat on her heels and pulled back her arm.

"Did you make it up?" Lisa demanded, looking at Jennifer's feet. And Jennifer realized Lisa had noticed her different-colored socks.

"No, I didn't make it all up!" Jennifer snapped. She opened her mouth to add, "I only made up part of it." But she couldn't. Lisa might stop being her friend . . . like everyone at school.

The two girls glared at each other. "Then Echo's dangerous!" Lisa yelled.

"And we're the only ones who know. So we'd better do something. Now!"

"Do something?" Jennifer asked. All at once, she was the one who felt like a frog—a little green and slimy, as if she'd landed with a big giant splat in a messy pond. "Do what?" she croaked.

7. Showdown at the Fence

Lisa's face looked as if it had been carved out of a rock. Jennifer had never seen her friend look so cold. She leaped on her bike and headed down the hill after her. Lisa must be planning something terrible. *Terrible.*

Jennifer could hear her father's voice in her mind, "Only little kids make up stories. When are you going to grow up?" Jennifer wished she'd never seen that umbrella. Then she wouldn't have been tempted to get so carried away. She hunched low over her handlebars and screeched around the corner to coast along their own flat street. Instantly, Lisa dropped back to ride beside her.

"Zoom!" Joshua scooted in between the

two girls. The whole world could be upset, and he wouldn't notice. They rode side by side, three in a row. Dad had better not come out of the house. She and Joshua were supposed to ride single file, and she was responsible for him, whether she liked it or not.

"Maybe the Catlady does voodoo," Lisa said. "Only she sticks umbrellas instead of pins into dolls." Her voice sounded so mean that Jennifer's insides twisted into knots.

They'd all been waiting dinosaur ages for Echo to do something ghastly. Like voodoo. And now . . . Jennifer shivered. She would just have to keep Lisa away from Echo until she cooled off. Then maybe she could convince her that Echo had been playing.

"Maybe it's one of us she wants to stab," Lisa said.

"She wants to stab YOU!" Joshua

veered gleefully toward Jennifer on the word *you*. Then he gasped. "What if she wants to stab Dad? Or Mom when she comes back?!"

Jennifer wished she could sink into the earth, bicycle and all. Echo was strange, crazy. But this wasn't even true. "Joshua—"

"I'll tell Dad," Joshua's voice shot way up high. He pedaled like an eggbeater to get ahead.

"You'll tell no one!" Lisa ordered.

Suddenly Joshua flung out his left arm to point and nearly hit Lisa in the chin. "There's the lady!"

Not now! Jennifer thought. She stopped so fast that she almost went over the handlebars. Lisa skidded sideways.

Echo balanced on the very top of her fence, six feet off the ground. She held the same bright green umbrella above her head with one hand. As they watched,

Echo took a step along the top, then another. She talked to herself, but Jennifer couldn't hear the words. Walking that fence was hard! Only Lisa had ever even tried it, and she could only do two steps before losing her balance.

Joshua scooted his bike behind Jennifer's. He held onto the back of her shirt so hard that her top button nearly strangled her.

The lady stepped forward again, then wobbled. She pressed the point of the umbrella down on the top of the fence for balance, like a dancer with a cane. But she only wobbled more. In slow motion, Echo toppled toward the children's side of the fence. She grabbed wildly for the top, and her cry changed to a screech. She landed half on her back in the rosebush.

Jennifer could imagine those prickly thorns stabbing into her own bottom. She raced forward.

"No, Jennifer!" Lisa cried.

"Remember the umbrella!" Joshua yelled.

But Echo looked like a helpless turtle stuck on its back. Jennifer had never been able to resist anything that looked helpless. She rushed on, then skidded to a stop before her. "Are you all right?"

Echo tried to right herself. "No, I'm not." She cradled her left hand, the one she had grabbed the fence with when she fell.

Jennifer shuffled forward. "Those thorns must hurt. Can I pull you out?" She held Echo's right arm and tugged. She yanked her halfway to her feet. Echo's clothing ripped.

Suddenly Lisa grabbed Jennifer and jerked her backward. "Get away from her!" Jennifer lost her grip on Echo's arm.

Echo wobbled, almost fell again, then regained her balance. She stared at Lisa, shocked. A part of Jennifer wanted to run screaming from the sudden anger in Echo's eyes.

Echo clenched her umbrella handle. "Jennifer tries to help me, and *you* tell her to get away?" She tapped Lisa gently on the chest with the tip of the umbrella.

Lisa's cheeks turned so pale that Jennifer thought she might faint. Joshua tugged on Jennifer's belt from behind. "Hurry! She'll stab us!"

"Stab you?" Echo exclaimed. Her face turned bright red. Jennifer backed up a step. Echo punched her umbrella tip into the ground by her feet. "Why, you *rude* children!"

Joshua screamed and ran. He fell flat on his face, hard, and kept screaming.

"He's only a little boy!" Jennifer glared at Echo. Lisa tugged her hand, but Jennifer wouldn't budge. She felt frozen, her feet glued to the ground. This couldn't be happening.

Echo poked at the air in front of the two girls. "First, you call me crazy. Then you run when I almost fall out of a tree!" She waved the umbrella over her head. "Now you accuse me of wanting to hurt you?"

Jennifer had never seen anyone look so furious. Lisa stumbled after Joshua.

Echo looked right at Jennifer. "Why don't you follow your friends?"

Because I want to talk! Jennifer screamed inside. *Because I want to know what you're really like.* But she couldn't get a single word out. *Why can't you just be normal?! Like neighbors are supposed to be?!*

Jennifer turned and ran after Lisa. She thought she heard the umbrella whistling through the air behind her.

Jennifer couldn't understand the rest of

Echo's words as she got closer to Joshua's screams. She yanked her little brother to his feet and dragged him along the sidewalk. He was shrieking so hard he could barely run.

As they climbed the porch steps, Jennifer glanced back. Echo was staring at them, one hand up to her mouth, the umbrella resting by her side. She looked as if she knew she'd done something terrible, as if she wanted to say she was sorry she had scared them.

The three children tumbled onto Jennifer and Joshua's front porch. Jennifer cradled Joshua against her. If he didn't stop howling he'd be sick. She was surprised Dad hadn't come out already.

"Now do you believe me?" Lisa pulled Jennifer around. She shoved Joshua's shoulders. "Be quiet!"

"Leave him alone!" Jennifer protected him with her arms. His cries made her feel sick inside. "Joshua. I'm here. It's okay."

"She . . . she . . . she tried to stab me!" Joshua stuttered. Jennifer could barely understand the words.

Lisa's face had changed to that carved rock again. "We have to take drastic steps." Lisa's icy voice dropped to a whisper. "We don't want that nasty lady living here anymore, do we?"

Jennifer twisted her head to look at the neighbor's house. Echo was walking in her gate, her shoulders hunched, dragging the umbrella by her side.

"DO WE?" Lisa cried, her cheeks purple.

Jennifer shivered in dismay. For once, she knew just how Echo felt.

8. Lisa's Plan

Jennifer didn't say good-bye. She raced up the stairs to her bedroom and slammed the door. She ignored Joshua's pounding moments later.

She *knew* Lisa was stomping home like a hippo hippopotamus, planning something dreadful against Echo. Jennifer crawled into bed, yanking her covers over her head. Joshua's footsteps retreated from her door as she drifted into a shocked sleep.

Jennifer awakened to see the afternoon shadows on her bed. She had missed lunch and slept almost until dinner.

Yet she didn't feel hungry.

The awful truth was as clear to Jennifer

as these shadows. If she hadn't exaggerated that story about the umbrella, Joshua wouldn't have been terrified of Echo. Lisa wouldn't have gotten so icy cold. Then Echo wouldn't have started yelling and waving the umbrella around. *None* of that scene would have happened.

Jennifer sat up, still groggy. If Mom were home, she would say that Jennifer couldn't change what she'd already done. So the question was, What should she do *now*?

Jennifer knew the answer. She should tell Lisa the truth, that all Echo had done was dance around her attic with an umbrella, pretending to sword fight.

But Lisa was her best friend, her *only* friend.

The phone rang. Jennifer tried to take a deep breath, but the air seemed to catch in her chest. She could stay inside and avoid Lisa. She could hope against hope that Lisa would forget, cool off. That's what she would do!

Footsteps climbed the stairs. "Jennifer?" Dad called softly. "The phone is for you."

Jennifer squeezed her covers. "Would you tell whoever it is that I'll call back later? Please? I'm . . . reading."

"The Professor at your service," Dad answered, in one of his funny voices.

Jennifer propped her chin on her stuffed rabbit. She'd better read a chapter in case Dad asked questions. The story reached out like a hook and pulled her inside. All evening she read *The Blue Cat of Castletown*. As usual, reading comforted her. Jennifer didn't stop until she finished at 9:15. She fell asleep with the book in her arms.

* * *

Sunday afternoon, Jennifer walked alone to the Corner Store. Luckily, Lisa had plans to visit her cousins all day.

Jennifer bought eight plastic bracelets, four different colors, with her allowance. She strolled home. When she climbed onto her porch, she could hear Dad and Joshua laughing inside.

"Look what I bought!" Jennifer burst in the door and waved her wrist. Joshua and Dad were building card houses.

Joshua's face lit up when he saw her.

The card building snaked halfway across the living room. Dad said, "When I was in grade school, all the guys wanted leather belts with their names on them."

Jennifer couldn't imagine the boys she knew wearing fancy leather belts to school.

Joshua had started building behind the couch. Jennifer could see his bottom sticking up in the air. He kept whispering, "Wombat, wombat."

"Your building is tremendous," Jennifer complimented them.

"Join us," Dad said. "We're creating a maze."

"No!" Joshua insisted. "It's a mouse house."

"How about an a*maz*ing mouse house?" Jennifer suggested. She grabbed a deck of cards with daisies on the back and began building a Gypsy's tent by the fireplace. It felt good to be playing with her family. Families lasted forever. . . . Jennifer wasn't so sure about friendships. She added a card for the roof, and the design collapsed. "Ooops."

They constructed apartment buildings, tents, A-frames, and malls for hours. Then they tiptoed into the kitchen. The slightest thump would make all the cards collapse.

Sunday was Scrounge Night at their house. That meant they each made their own dinner. She and Joshua heated up a pizza, and Dad made himself a giant salad. Mom liked to tease Dad that if he wasn't careful, he'd turn into a rabbit.

Jennifer was stretching the cheese off her pizza with her teeth when the phone rang. Dad answered. "Hi, Lisa."

No, Dad, Jennifer thought as hard as she could. *Don't let me talk to her.*

Dad shook his head, as if Lisa could see him, "Sorry, Lisa McRollovitch. We're eating dinner. No, she can't play later. It's a school night, remember?"

Dad hung up. Jennifer stared at her plate, but she could feel her father's eyes on her. "If something is wrong, Jennifer, you can talk to me."

He leaned across the table and patted her other hand. He ruffled Joshua's hair, too. "I don't know how to say this, but I feel as though I have my children back." He squeezed her fingers. "I'm glad you two chose to have a quiet day with me instead of playing in the attic."

Jennifer finally smiled. "Me, too," she whispered. Being with her dad and Joshua had made her feel as if she could truly breathe again.

To Jennifer's relief, Dad didn't ask any more questions.

Monday morning arrived. Jennifer bit her lip as she waited for Lisa to walk to school. Joshua played hopscotch on the sidewalk.

When Lisa arrived, she lowered her voice dramatically. "Friday is Halloween, right? I made up a plan called Halloween Echo. The night before Halloween we sneak out of our houses and leave Echo notes telling her how we feel about her. Maybe we could squash a few plants, too."

"Like creeping into a graveyard!" Joshua exclaimed.

Jennifer shivered. Not seeing Lisa for the weekend hadn't done any good at all. In fact, her worst fears had come true! She could tell that Lisa was waiting for her reaction.

Lisa added details to her scheme as they walked. "The real plan is for the next night, Halloween. We'll scare Echo so badly she'll move right out and never want to come back. We'll string a giant skeleton across her front yard on a rope." Lisa sounded almost bubbly. "She'll think the skeleton is *haunting* her."

Three times, Jennifer opened her mouth to interrupt Lisa with the truth about the umbrella. She felt like a baby bird, opening her mouth and shutting it again.

At her classroom door, Jennifer fished her new plastic bracelets out of her pocket. She hadn't wanted Lisa to see them. She slipped the three greens and two reds onto her right wrist, alternating the colors. Then she surrounded the purple with the two blues on her left wrist. She hurried to her desk. Wearing the bracelets made her feel shy.

During magazine time, Betsy leaned toward her. "I love your greens and reds!" she whispered.

Betsy's eyes seemed to be pleading with her to be friendly. Jennifer wanted to believe that Betsy still liked her. Jennifer looked at her desk. Maybe Betsy just didn't know how to resist Shannon. Shannon was awfully popular and pushy. So Jennifer wrote a note:

Dear Betsy,
Can you imagine a black cat
wearing tiny green and red
bracelets around its tail?
J.

The note was silly, but it was the best she could do. Jennifer passed the note.

During the next two days, Jennifer wished every morning and night and probably two hundred times in between that she'd never made up that story about Echo stabbing the dummy with an umbrella. Then they would have all gone on having fun spying on Echo, not making up a PLAN.

Each day, Lisa gleefully added something a bit more gruesome to Halloween Echo. Lisa decided that she would dress up all in black, and swing on the rope above the skeleton and drop worms all over Echo. Joshua would moan and throw eggs at the windows. To get Echo outside, Jennifer would lie on her path pretending to be injured. They would use ketchup for fake blood to make a ghastly scene. Grown-ups hated the sight of blood.

Joshua acted as if he'd been lit up by a light bulb, he had so much energy. He never let Lisa get more than two feet away from him. And the little twerp didn't even notice how upset Jennifer felt.

"Are you sick?" Dad asked Jennifer at dinner Wednesday night. He twisted his beard to make her laugh. "This is ham. See? With brown sugar . . . the way you like it."

Jennifer shook her head silently. She couldn't eat.

Thursday morning, the day before Halloween, Jennifer grew even quieter. She felt like a robot. But she wore the bracelets to school. That afternoon after school, she even helped Lisa write the nasty notes. The notes said things like, *Move out, crazy lady*; *Horrible hateful hag*; *Dragons need feet, too*; *Fly to your roof, fly away*; and *No one wants you living here.*

Now, they were all ready . . . ready for the night to come.

9. Night in the Garden

At 9:31, thirty-one minutes after Jennifer's bedtime and sixty-one minutes after Joshua's, she and her brother crept down the stairs in their pajamas and jackets. Dad sat reading in the big easy chair in the living room, ten feet from the bottom of the stairs. What if he looked over his shoulder? Jennifer led the way, crawling across the back of the dining room into the kitchen. She unlatched the back door and watched Joshua turn into a shadow boy in the darkness. She slipped out after him and pulled the door closed.

Joshua let out a giant breath as if he were blowing out a birthday cake. His breath sailed in front of him like smoke.

They sat down together to pull on their tennis shoes. For once, Jennifer was glad of her pesky little brother's company.

Lisa waited under the oak tree in the inky darkness. Solemnly, she handed them each a thick stick. The stick seemed big to Jennifer. All they were supposed to do was smash a *few* plants. No one said a word. The three children tiptoed along the front of the fence and through Echo's gate.

Last of all, Jennifer peered into the garden. Lisa glanced back, watching her. Like a robot, Jennifer pretended to swing her stick at the nearest rosebush. Then she watched in horror as the stick connected, and a single rose fell.

On the other side of the yard, Jennifer could already hear Joshua slashing at the snapdragons and trampling the purple flowers. He must be destroying everything. Echo's beautiful garden . . . all

dying. Jennifer dropped the stick as if it had burned her.

What was she doing here?!

She didn't want to scare Echo into moving away and never coming back. She wanted to ignore the crazy lady, never talk to her, pretend she didn't even live next door.

Jennifer glanced at the windows of the house. Perhaps Echo was sitting there in the darkness right now, watching. Jennifer shivered. Why hadn't she told Lisa NO, that she wouldn't destroy Echo's garden?

Jennifer's hands felt like sweaty ice cubes. She *never* said no to Lisa. Never. Never. Never. Last week she'd disobeyed the rule about riding bikes single file, she'd made up those hateful notes this afternoon, and now here she was in Echo's yard. She hadn't wanted to do any of those things. Yet she'd done them . . . because Lisa was her friend.

Lisa disappeared around the corner of Echo's house, swinging madly with her stick.

In the moonlight, Jennifer saw her little brother stomp on a tiny bush and break it to the ground. Joshua was such a little boy to be doing something so vicious. *Vicious* was their vocabulary word for the week. It meant cruel. Jennifer imagined Joshua grown, seven feet tall, skinny and vicious. Would he still enjoy destroying things that weren't his?

Jennifer suddenly knew she had to do something. She rushed across the yard and grabbed her little brother's arm. "We're going home. Do you want to grow up to be vicious?"

Joshua looked up, startled. "What?"

Jennifer dragged him toward the gate.

"I don't want to go." Joshua squashed another flower. "Echo is a witch." He kicked her in the shins, hard.

"Echo is not a witch," Jennifer exclaimed, wincing in pain. Joshua hadn't kicked her like that in years.

Lisa came around the side of the house.

Jennifer held onto her brother so hard that she could feel the bones of his arm. She had to dance out of the way of his kicking feet. Clearly, she couldn't force him. "Joshua, please do what I want you to do. This is wrong." Jennifer was choking back tears, so her next words came out even more fiercely, "You're my little brother. I *love* you."

Joshua stopped kicking. His voice sounded like a tiny boy's. "Jennifer?"

Lisa caught up with them. "Where are you going?"

Neither of them answered. "Then come on!" Lisa demanded. "We haven't stuck the notes onto bushes yet."

Jennifer felt her face grow hot with embarrassment when she thought of the notes. With a deep breath, she faced her friend. She was so upset, her legs quivered. "You do it," she whispered. Now was the time she'd tell Lisa NO. She would say it right to her face for the first time in her whole life.

"Coward." Lisa clenched her hands into fists. "I'll do the rest alone, then. I don't need your help. You'll see."

"I'll help!" Joshua cried loudly.

"Be quiet!" Both girls hissed at the same instant. Jennifer felt as if her heart had stopped beating. Now she and Lisa were supposed to tap foreheads. Since the first grade, they had tapped foreheads every time they'd said something together. Jennifer backed up a step. She couldn't do it. Not tonight.

"I know I heard something," Dad's voice suddenly exclaimed from Jennifer and Joshua's front yard. "Do you suppose someone's there?"

"Seeeee?" she whispered, hating herself before the words came out. "I told you we have to go."

Lisa nodded, trust back in her eyes. "Go on," she mouthed. "I'll finish."

Joshua tugged Jennifer this time. The two of them ran out of the gate and along the front of Echo's fence. Jennifer felt a wave of panic washing over her. Dad and the neighbor from across the street stood on the far side of the porch. "Maybe it was over here," the neighbor said.

Jennifer jerked on her brother's hand so hard that she almost pulled him off his feet. Now was their chance. They ran down their side yard.

"I'm sure I heard a sound by Echo's house," Dad said firmly. "There it is now!"

Jennifer ran even faster. She and Joshua reached the back just as all the lights in the yard flashed on. Her father flung open the back door. Jennifer pulled her brother down on the back step. Dad rushed down the stairs so fast that he almost fell over them. "What are you doing here?"

"We're . . ." Jennifer hesitated. She tried not to pant. "We're looking at the stars." Joshua leaned against her. He was trembling.

"Did you hear something?" Dad demanded suspiciously.

"Something ran that way," Jennifer said.

"A . . . a dog!" Joshua exclaimed. Jennifer squeezed his leg proudly. Her brother was growing old enough to learn how to cover up. Then she stopped her hand in the middle of a pat. Her brother was learning how to *lie* . . . just like her.

Her father leaned his head around the side of the house. "Herb? It's just my kids and a dog. See you tomorrow." Then he came back and sat down on the step beside them. He put his arm around Jennifer. "Tell me, why are you outside?"

Jennifer suddenly felt like sobbing. She didn't want to lie to her Dad. But if she didn't, he would find out what had happened. "It was a game," she said as cheerfully as she could. She couldn't even look at Dad. "I wanted to show Joshua the North Star. We learned about it in school today." She felt relieved to say at least one thing true. "We couldn't find it."

Dad sighed. "I'll be glad when Halloween is over. Then maybe you'll stop being so excited and doing absurd things. You know I don't like you coming out after your bedtime. Next time you'll be punished. Do you understand?"

"Yes, sir," Jennifer muttered.

Joshua crawled into Dad's lap, and Dad wrapped his long arms around him. "You're trembling."

"Cold." Joshua cuddled against Dad's bony shoulder.

Dad pointed into the sky. "See those

four stars that look like a pot and then the three that look like a handle?"

Joshua shook his head. "I see a square cat with a crooked tail."

"That's the Big Dipper," her father continued. "Now . . ."

As soon as she could, Jennifer slipped away. Tonight had been only the beginning. Lisa would hate her if she refused to participate tomorrow.

If only Mom were home. Jennifer crawled into bed. She couldn't ask Dad for advice. How could she explain to him that she had spied on Echo and made up *another* story? Jennifer felt heartsick. Dad had already told her to grow up. If he knew what she had just done, he'd be sure she was only a little girl, a mean little girl.

A hand dropped onto her back, and Jennifer jumped. "Something wrong, love?"

Her father tucked her in, for the second time that night.

Jennifer shook her head. "I'm just tired."

"It's too late for you to be up." Dad pulled her door closed. "Sleep tight."

"Night, Dad." Jennifer buried her face in the pillow. She thought of Lisa out in the night right now tying a rope in a tree. Then she thought of her little brother jumping up and smashing a tiny plant under his feet. She only had twenty-four hours, twenty-four hours to come up with her own plan to stop Halloween Echo.

10. Only Seven More Hours

Jennifer removed her bracelets from her backpack and set them out on her desk in a neat row. She'd spent the entire morning at school thinking about tonight. Now she only had seven more hours before Halloween Echo began. To her dismay Jennifer had realized that even if she told Lisa the truth about the umbrella, tonight wouldn't be stopped. Lisa was enjoying herself too much. Even if she refused to help, Lisa and Joshua could do most of the plan by themselves.

Jennifer picked up a green bracelet. She'd gone along with wearing these bracelets so that she'd be like her classmates, so they wouldn't think she was odd.

And she'd gone along with Halloween Echo so her best friend wouldn't get mad at her.

Jennifer pulled her scissors out of her desk. She didn't want to be *exactly* the same as everyone else, even if people would like her more.

She opened the scissors and inserted the bracelet between the sharp blades. . . . But no, she couldn't make herself cut the bracelet into little pieces. She liked the greenness. Jennifer sighed. Maybe it didn't hurt to go along with a fashion if she liked it, as long as she didn't hurt other people or make fun of them. Even Dad had said that his friends used to have fads.

But going along with Halloween Echo . . . well, that was different. Someone could get hurt, and it would be her fault. If she didn't do something, she would *hate* herself.

She might as well wear a sign around her neck for the rest of her life that said:

JENNIFER

The Coward
She could never say no.

The Liar
She turned her little brother into a villain.

The One Who Makes Up Stories
She stayed a ratty little kid all her life.

Forever Unpopular

During the last hour of school, an answer finally oozled into Jennifer's mind. The idea could succeed. There was even a chance things might work out with Lisa. Jennifer slipped a piece of lined paper on top of her Halloween art project and started to write. *Dear Echo.* She crossed out the *Dear*.

Echo,
Something terrible is going to happen. . . .

Jennifer wrote steadily for half an hour. Then she folded the two-page note and put it carefully in her pocket.

If Lisa found out she had written this note, she would never talk to her again. What would it be like to live on the block without Lisa as a friend?

When the bell rang, Jennifer grabbed her jacket and hurried from the building. She felt sorry to leave Joshua, but she didn't have a choice.

Perhaps she should leave the note on Echo's front porch, rather than in the mailbox. Echo *had* to read the note tonight. Jennifer crouched and ran behind the parked cars as she drew close to Echo's house. Finally, she peered through the open gate. Echo's bicycle rested against the porch railing. She must be home.

Jennifer pulled the note out of her pocket. Her hands trembled so badly that she dropped it. Quickly, Jennifer picked up the note and dashed up the path. She couldn't hear anything except her own heartbeat.

On the porch, Jennifer stopped. All around the yard lay trampled bushes and limp flower blossoms. Jennifer gulped, closed her eyes. She hadn't imagined it would look so terrible.

Jennifer leaned over to put the note on the doormat. Now she had to ring the doorbell and wait three seconds until Echo had left the front window. Then she would race out the gate. Jennifer stood up, lifted her finger toward the doorbell. She felt dizzy.

The door flew open. Echo looked twice as big as she usually did. Jennifer gasped.

"You!" Echo pointed her finger, as Dad did when he was furious. "You children ruined my flowers!"

Jennifer felt as if her shoes were nailed to the front porch. Echo wasn't supposed to know who had destroyed her garden. It could have been anyone. Jennifer forced herself to shuffle backward. She would run.

Echo grabbed her wrist. "And you left those notes." Her voice cracked.

Jennifer could feel the woman's pain in her own chest.

"I loved those flowers!" Echo wailed, releasing Jennifer and waving at the garden.

Jennifer looked sadly around the yard again, then up at Echo's green eyes.

Suddenly Jennifer *knew* with absolute certainty that this woman wasn't dangerous or even crazy. She was just very, very different from anyone she had ever met before.

Jennifer leaned down to pick up the note. She handed it to Echo. Then she followed the woman blindly into the house.

Jennifer sat on the very edge of a chair in the living room, while Echo put on her glasses to read. Jennifer opened her mouth to say that she hadn't destroyed any of Echo's flowers. Then she closed it again, remembering the one red rose.

Echo stopped reading the note and looked at her. "Tonight? This is all going to happen tonight?"

Jennifer nodded.

Echo stood up suddenly and went into the kitchen. She came back with two glasses in her hands. She shoved one at Jennifer. "Then you have a great deal to tell me."

Jennifer couldn't drink the purple juice, but holding the glass felt good. She started at the beginning. Once again she had the feeling of being a robot, in a haze deep within herself. She told Echo about the spying and about seeing her singing to the moon. Jennifer stumbled over her words, and her voice came out squeaky. Yet she continued. Echo sat still. When Jennifer got to the part about making up the story about the umbrella, she felt so ashamed that she almost started crying.

Echo giggled or at least snorted. Startled, Jennifer really looked at the Catlady for the first time since she'd entered the house.

"I used to exaggerate myself when I was a kid," Echo explained. "Everyone got so mad at me."

Jennifer had never heard a grown-up talk like this. "Then you don't think that only *little* kids make up stories?"

"Who told you that?" Echo asked softly. Her eyes looked friendly.

Jennifer clamped one hand over her mouth and shook her head. Then she whispered, "My dad."

"No, I don't agree with him. But people

have different opinions. Your father is a very nice man."

"You know my father?" Jennifer exclaimed.

Echo laughed. "I *am* his neighbor."

Jennifer cleared her throat. Would she ever stop being startled by this woman?

How could Echo do such odd things and yet be so friendly? Echo even had a statue on her mantle of a little girl petting a goat. A dragon kite with a long colorful tail had been tacked over the doorway into the kitchen. A bird cage with a canary inside hung from one corner. And she had books everywhere, just like Jennifer's house.

Echo gazed at her solemnly. "Go on."

Jennifer had no doubt that Echo would know exactly what was the truth. So she didn't exaggerate one bit. By the time Jennifer got to the horrible plans for tonight, she could hardly talk. She told Echo about her part—the fake injury—and what Lisa was going to do, and Joshua.

"So Lisa made up this plan, and you followed her?" Echo asked. "You didn't even argue?"

Jennifer nodded miserably.

"You three did all this because you think I'm 'weird,' as you put it?" Echo's eyes begged Jennifer to argue, to give another reason. But Jennifer couldn't. She nodded again.

The woman stared at her silently. "Why do people hate people who are different?" Echo finally whispered. "Even children hate." Then to Jennifer's horror, Echo burst into tears.

11. Halloween

Jennifer slipped into Joshua's room after dinner. She hadn't been able to catch him alone all afternoon. He'd been helping Dad set up the house for Halloween. Joshua was tugging his dragon costume on over his green sweat suit.

"Promise you won't tell?" Jennifer asked, leaning against the closed door. Joshua crossed his heart eagerly. He loved secrets. "I talked to Echo this afternoon, Joshua," Jennifer said. "I went into her house."

Joshua gasped. "Did she try to stab you?"

"She gave me grape juice." Her little brother liked juice. "Joshua, you know what? I think Echo might be friendly." He looked disbelieving. She didn't blame him. It was hard for her to believe when she wasn't in Echo's home.

The doorbell rang. Then Jennifer could hear Lisa's voice downstairs. She had hoped she would have more time to talk to Joshua.

Jennifer helped her little brother pull on the dragon's head. She handed him his empty Halloween pumpkin for his candy. "What we did last night was *wrong*, Joshua. So, we're just going trick or treating tonight. We're going to leave Echo alone!"

"What about our plan?" Joshua stomped his foot as he did when something wasn't fair. "Does Lisa know?!"

"Not yet." Jennifer opened his door. "And *you* promised not to tell her I talked to Echo."

Jennnifer slipped her sheet over her head and arranged the eyes. Because of

Halloween Echo, she had agreed to dress as a ghost. Lisa got to be the black cat, since she needed to be dark to play her part.

Lisa stood at the bottom of the stairs, pulling a cardboard skeleton from her bag. She wore a black sweater, gloves, and a dark green hood with small gray cat ears. Her face had been blackened with charcoal. A long tail looped over her shoulder.

Lisa had painted the skeleton all black. She had attached strips of bright orange tape that would glow in the dark. She had even put spots of orange on the face. The skeleton stood taller than Lisa. "I hooked tin cans to the feet so it would rattle."

Suddenly, Jennifer found herself remembering how much she liked Lisa. Her friend was good at doing so much, like running and bicycling and creating such terrific things.

"That's wonderful," Jennifer said shyly.

Joshua bounded down the last steps, pointing. "Wow!"

"Thanks, Dragonsquirt." Then Lisa winked at Jennifer. "Ready?"

"Sure, she's ready." Dad reached out and put his arm around Jennifer. "My little Halloween ghost. I wish your mother could be here." The jaw of Dad's black Death mask moved when he talked.

Dad wore a black robe with a hood that nearly covered his mask. He wore a necklace of bones. He told everybody they were kids' fingers, but Jennifer knew they were chicken bones. No matter how many times Jennifer saw that costume, it gave her the shivers.

Jennifer hurried past the life-size plastic monster by the front door. " 'Bye, Dad!"

"Have a marvelously wicked Halloween!" Dad called in his scary Death voice.

He closed the door behind them. Jennifer could hear the eerie Halloween music begin to play. Tonight every trick or treater would have to walk into the dark kitchen alone with Death to get the Professor's famous bag of candy.

The instant the door closed Joshua puffed himself up like a fat proud dragon. "Jennifer and I have a secret." Jennifer sent him a look that should have turned him into dust. His shoulders slumped. "I didn't tell the secret," he whined.

Lisa leaned over to tie her tennis shoe, as if she hadn't heard. Jennifer faced her friend. "Lisa?" Now was the time to speak.

Lisa stood up and rubbed her palms together excitedly. "Let's get started."

Lisa had a horrible habit of ignoring what she didn't want to hear. Jennifer walked forward until she stood eye to eye with her friend. "We can't do Halloween

Echo. We can't!" Jennifer's knees trembled, but she felt excitement rushing through her. She had said no to Lisa!

Lisa stepped back calmly. "Getting chicken?" She didn't yell or anything. "Joshua's not scared. Are you?"

Joshua looked anxiously at Jennifer. Three little pigs and a wolf turned down the end of their street, headed their way.

"Are you?" Lisa almost snarled.

"No," he whispered.

Jennifer clenched her hands into fists. "It's just . . ." She remembered Echo's face when she had burst into tears. "We already destroyed Echo's flowers. How would you like it if someone ruined something of yours?" Jennifer couldn't ever remember talking back to Lisa this much.

"We want her to leave," Lisa whispered in a creepy voice. "Remember? We're doing the neighborhood a favor. She's weird and crazy and *dangerous.*"

Jennifer put her hands on her hips. "No, she's not!"

"How do you know?" Lisa asked in a singsong voice.

"Because I talked to her! Echo isn't—" Jennifer clamped her lips shut. She hadn't meant to say that much.

"Liar," Lisa said scornfully. "You didn't talk to her."

Jennifer felt like tromping Lisa's toes flat. "I did see her. I knocked on her door. Echo has never hurt one of us. We've exaggerated everything."

"Liar, liar, pants on fire," Lisa sang.

Joshua giggled.

Suddenly, Jennifer grew icy cold inside. She had a wonderfully horrid thought. Maybe they *should* go ahead with Halloween Echo. Maybe pushy old Lisa should get exactly what she wanted . . . since she wouldn't listen. Echo already knew what was going to happen. Jennifer had warned her, so she wouldn't really be scared.

And who knew what ghastly things might happen to Lisa?

12. Trick or Treat

Lisa swung easily into the tree in Jennifer's side yard and untied the rope. "Hand me the skeleton," she ordered.

Jennifer held the skeleton up to Lisa, but not quite close enough for her to reach. Lisa leaned, stretching closer with her black cat fingertips. At the last moment, Jennifer yanked the skeleton away. She didn't care how angry Lisa got.

Lisa wobbled, almost falling out of the tree. "Turkey," she hissed. Darting forward, she snatched the skeleton from Jennifer's hand. Lisa tied the head of the skeleton to the rope. The other end of the rope was already tied to a high branch of the oak tree in Echo's yard . . . the same tree Echo had nearly fallen out of so long ago. The branch spread right over Echo's front walk.

"Go on," Lisa said to Jennifer, her voice steely. "Do your part right."

Jennifer dragged Joshua around to Echo's front gate. Do it right? What was that supposed to mean? That Lisa thought she would botch this? Hah! Was Lisa in for a surprise!

The three little pigs and the bad wolf went by on the sidewalk toward Jennifer's porch. Good, that would keep Dad occupied for a while.

Jennifer peered inside Echo's gate. The front porch light was on, ready for trick or treaters. "Do you have your branches, Joshua?" He nodded. He held out the eggs. "Forget those," Jennifer told him. "They'll make a mess on Echo's windows." She pulled a bottle of ketchup out of her bag and squeezed half the ketchup over her left arm.

Joshua dropped the eggs right there on the sidewalk, and they oozed into a pool of muck. "You said tonight was wrong. Then you just *ordered* me to go ahead with the plan." Joshua sounded confused, as if he might cry.

"Joshua . . ." Jennifer felt her fury seeping out of her. Joshua hadn't really told Lisa their secret tonight. He had just hinted. As Mom said, he was still awfully little. Jennifer wanted to throw her arms around him, but that would make him all red, too. Jennifer wiped her hand on the white sheet. Now her costume looked good and gory.

"Just stay close to me, Joshua. No matter what. And don't do anything mean to Echo. I'll explain later."

Jennifer put her hand on Joshua's shoulder. "Let's go!" she whispered, giving him a little push. Side by side, they sneaked into Echo's yard. Jennifer closed the wooden gate behind them. She hoped no other trick or treaters would come with the gate latched. Joshua tiptoed alone to the side of the house. She could hardly see him.

Halloween Echo was finally beginning, and she had the first move. Jennifer felt a tingle of excitement rushing through her. She'd never done a Halloween trick before. Halfway to the house, Jennifer pulled a fake hand out of her jeans pocket and squirted ketchup over it, too. She lay down on the path and set the rubbery hand on her stomach, hiding her real hand under the sheet.

Jennifer looked at the tree where Lisa nestled in the shadows. She still hoped that something horrid would happen to her. Jennifer heard the front door of her house creak open. The three little pigs and a squealing wolf scurried down the street toward Lisa's.

Next, Jennifer searched until she saw the shadow of Joshua crouched in the bushes. He was ready.

So was she.

This night would change her. In the Halloween moonlight, Jennifer thought about school. She knew she wouldn't behave in a certain way because of Shannon ever again. Shannon was just a bully, even if she was popular. But Jennifer could feel that something else about her was going to change tonight, and she didn't know what.

Jennifer took a deep breath. These next few minutes needed to be the best acting she'd ever done in her life! Jennifer began to scream. She kicked her feet on the sidewalk and rolled from side to side and *yelled*.

The front door of the house flew open. Echo stood silhouetted in the doorway. She wore a long gown and a tightly fitting black cap. Somehow that cap was more frightening than a pointed hat would have been. She was a witch.

Jennifer felt as if someone had thrown a bucket of cold water over her face. She hesitated in mid-scream. Should she not have gone ahead with the plan?!

Echo rushed forward and knelt beside Jennifer, her eyes fierce. She looked completely different from how she had looked that afternoon.

"Keep screaming, you silly idiot," Echo said under her breath.

Jennifer swallowed and nearly grinned. Echo *was* pretending. "My hand!" Jennifer yelled. "My hand!"

"Oh, how *hideous*." Echo's voice slid upwards to a loud wail. "Poor Jennifer." Then she turned her face away and whispered nastily, "A child for my experiment."

Joshua gasped so loudly that Jennifer heard him. She also heard the rattling skeleton. Jennifer pretended to sob.

Echo wrapped the fake hand up in her gown. "Maybe the hospital can sew this back on for you." She put her hand under Jennifer's arm and lifted her. "Come, child."

Lisa suddenly came sailing across the yard on the rope, her feet resting on the big knot. She was nearly invisible in the darkness. The skeleton dangled beneath her.

"Depart," a deep voice boomed, as if from the bony body of the skeleton. The skeleton rattled across the path only a few feet from Jennifer and Echo. "Go away forever." The voice didn't sound like Lisa's at all.

The skeleton looked frightening, really scary. So far their plan was working beautifully.

Echo froze, then set Jennifer down. "Me? Go away?"

Jennifer could hear Joshua rattling his branches across the windows of Echo's house and moaning.

"Or I will haunt you," Lisa intoned as she swooped across the rest of the yard. "Forever."

Echo screamed. She sounded terrified. Jennifer suddenly realized that Echo was magnificent at pretending like this. Maybe she was an actor.

Lisa swung backward. "Blood!" she cried. Now it was time for her to squeeze her sponge and dribble warm ketchup all over them. A giant splat landed on Echo's face as the skeleton rattled across Jennifer's feet. "Death!" Lisa intoned. Sticky worms landed on the sidewalk. One hit Echo on the nose.

Jennifer had forgotten to tell Echo about the worms.

Echo leaped backward, her arms stretched into the air. "Leave us, bag of bones!" she yelled at the skeleton.

Jennifer stumbled to her feet, scared despite herself. Joshua ran out of the shadows. Now they were supposed to run out the gate while Echo was busy with the skeleton. Lisa would grab hold of the branch as she swung back. Then she would disappear down the tree. Their entire plan had worked perfectly.

But Jennifer didn't move. Lisa was fumbling, pulling something else out of the bag that dangled around her neck. What was she doing? Lisa threw an object toward Echo's front window. Jennifer gasped. Lisa hadn't said anything about a rock. Echo screamed, one hand over her chest, as the rock flew toward her window and . . .

. . . and bounced off the frame.

Echo took a deep hissing breath, the way Mom did when she was really mad. She stood taller and started chanting, *"Black cat*, *skeleton's cap* . . ."

Joshua threw his arms around Jennifer's waist. They both watched Lisa swing back toward their tree. She couldn't get turned around right. Wildly, she lunged for her branch, and *missed.* She stifled her exclamation as she swung backward, right toward Echo's outstretched arms.

"*Skeleton's cap*," Echo repeated. Her voice sounded like a bass drum. The black-and-orange skeleton bumped into her shoulder. Echo snatched her black cap off and flipped it onto the skeleton's head.

"*Black cat, skeleton's cap*," Jennifer repeated in a whisper.

"It's a spell!" Joshua screeched.

Jennifer caught a glimpse of Lisa's horrified face.

Echo raised her hands above her head. "*Bring the spirit to where I'm at!*" Echo waited until Lisa swung by. Then with a triumphant cry, she leaped out and grabbed the rope beneath Lisa's feet. Lisa screamed. Both of her feet slipped off the knot, and she almost fell.

"Run!" Joshua yelled, but he didn't let go of Jennifer. She held on to his shoulders, hard.

Echo grabbed Lisa's waist and helped her down. "Come into my house, Black Cat." She turned to the others and looked into each of their eyes. "Not one child, but three." Then she laughed, a high cackling witch's laugh. "My experiment awaits."

13. Echo's Experiment

Echo closed her front door and flipped off the porch light. "We wouldn't want any more trick or treaters disturbing us." Burning candles had been arranged on the dining room table. They flickered eerily in the dark room. Joshua pulled off his dragon's head.

Echo turned to Lisa. "What animal would *you* like to be turned into for my experiment? A rhinoceros, perhaps? Lovely pet, though they are a bit hard on gardens."

"Don't be silly," Lisa snapped. She edged toward the door. "I'll tell my mom."

"A fearful lion, I believe . . ." Echo lifted Lisa's chin with one finger. "All roar until someone stands up to you."

Lisa shoved her hands into her pockets as she always did when she was trying to look calm. "I'm *not* scared."

"To the kitchen then, Brave One." Echo pointed the way through the doorway under the dragon kite.

Next, Echo spun around to stare at Jennifer. Jennifer stumbled back, her mouth dry. Echo folded her arms. "You'll be a fox, I think. Cunning. Always looking for the quiet way to do something. A bit sneaky."

"But!" Jennifer exclaimed. She stopped arguing when Echo gave her a searing look. Well, maybe she was a little sneaky. But foxes were clever, too. And wild. And beautiful. It wasn't such a bad thing to be.

Echo knelt in front of Joshua. "And you're dressed as something brave. Would you like to be a real dragon?"

Joshua looked up at Echo, gasped, and let out an ear-splitting howl. "You can't have my feet for your lucky charms!"

Echo sat back on her heels, startled. Jennifer could tell from Echo's face that, for a moment, she'd stopped acting. The woman held out her hand to reassure Joshua, but he skittered around to Jennifer's back. "You'll be a fox, like your sister."

Echo stood up, back in character. "Come now. To the kitchen." She pushed Lisa gently out of the room.

Jennifer leaned her head down close to her little brother's ear so only he could hear. "Echo is only pretending, Joshua. Remember? She's not dangerous."

Joshua sniffed. "Let's go! Out the door!"

"If you dally, I'll turn you both into rats," Echo said, sticking her head back into the dining room.

Jennifer pulled Joshua into the kitchen. If she let him leave she'd have to go with him. She wouldn't miss this for anything.

Echo's performance was the best she'd ever seen.

The brightness in the kitchen made Jennifer blink. Then she saw the cooking pot and stopped in amazement. "Jeepers, creepers! What's that?"

A giant pot bubbled on the stove. The biggest wooden spoon that Jennifer had ever seen stuck out of the top. Little black bottles had been lined up across the counter.

Jennifer leaned closer to the bottles. One of the labels said *Frog Legs*. She glanced at Lisa standing sullenly in the center of the room and couldn't resist reading another label aloud, "*Little Boys' Toes*."

Echo motioned Lisa to stand beside the steaming pot. "You first."

Lisa never denied a dare. She stepped closer. The room became so silent that Jennifer couldn't hear breathing, not even

Joshua's. Echo poured in a few flakes from a jar labeled, "*Dried Chameleon.*" Then she chanted,

"*Bubbling vat,*
Help me CHANGE
Lisa into a giant *scaredy-cat.*"

Lisa's cheeks blanched whiter. Echo stirred the pot with the giant wooden spoon in a witchy way. Jennifer swallowed.

Echo fished a cloth out of the pot.

"*Changing colors!*"

In the steamy air above the pot, the cloth changed color from yellow to blue! Right in front of their eyes!

Jennifer stumbled. She saw Lisa hold herself up against the countertop. The cloth changed again, first to green, then to red. Echo waved the steaming cloth over the top of Lisa's head.

"Swirling child!
Let Lisa become
An animal wild."

"I don't want to be a fox," Joshua screeched. "I don't want my toes in a jar!"

Jennifer held on to her wiggling little brother.

"Change now!" Echo cried in a firm voice. Lisa started to run. A poof of steam rose from the pot as the room plunged into darkness.

Jennifer felt her little brother's panic through her fingertips. She heard her own gasp as if it were coming from a different person. Then she heard a *crash*.

"Lisa? Are you all right?!" Jennifer cried into the blackness. Why didn't Lisa answer? She couldn't have really changed into a lion . . . could she?!

The lights in the kitchen flipped back

on. Jennifer dashed forward. She dragged Joshua along with her since he wouldn't let go of her ghostly sheet. The sheet ripped and her head poked out the top. Jennifer didn't see any signs of lion fur on Lisa's face. Her friend didn't have any sharp teeth.

Jennifer crouched and put her hand on Lisa's arm. "Did you hurt yourself?" She'd been furious all day at Lisa, but now her anger had vanished.

"She's insane!" Lisa untangled her legs from a chair. In all the years they'd been friends, Jennifer had never known Lisa to howl like a five-year-old. "Echo is crazy!"

"She's not crazy now," Joshua whispered.

Jennifer looked up, startled. Echo stood by the kitchen door, her black robe folded neatly over one arm. She wore blue jeans and a purple sweatshirt. Jennifer could see one purple and one blue sock peeking over her black shoes.

"I've always wanted to play that scene," Echo said, smiling.

Lisa sat up, her back straight. "What?!"

For a minute, Jennifer had forgotten that Echo was pretending. She picked up the chair and sat down, her knees trembling. Joshua still didn't let go of her.

"That scene will be perfect in my book," Echo said, rummaging around in her cupboard. "Would you like some herbal tea or orange juice?"

"What?" Lisa exclaimed again. She stood up beside Jennifer's chair. Her cheeks were turning bright red.

"I offered you tea or orange juice," Echo replied in a very polite voice. "I don't have any 'what.' "

Joshua peered out from behind Jennifer's chair. He had ketchup smeared in his hair and down the front of his costume. Jennifer had not seen him so messy in years. "Orange juice for me!" Joshua squeaked, then hid behind her again.

"In your book?" Jennifer asked.

"You mean all of this was a trick?" Lisa interrupted, her fists on her hips. "You scared us on purpose?!"

"Wasn't it your idea to scare me?" Echo calmly closed the refrigerator door. "You squeezed ketchup on my face and dropped worms on my head." Echo looked sternly at each of them. "And you ruined *my flowers!*"

Joshua poked at the linoleum with his tennis shoe. Jennifer felt so embarrassed that her eyes tingled. But Lisa . . . Lisa glared right back at Echo.

"You didn't only want to scare me, either." Echo sounded hurt. "Jennifer told me you wanted me to leave forever. What have I ever done to you?"

Lisa leaped away from Jennifer's side as if she'd been burned. "You *told* her our plan?"

Jennifer had truly never seen Lisa look that upset. Jennifer stared back at her, speechless.

"How could you?" Lisa cried.

Jennifer knew she had to say something. "I . . . " Her voice came out as hardly a whisper. ". . . couldn't make you stop."

"You knew all this was going to happen?" Lisa waved her arm in a sweeping motion, then pointed at Echo. "You let *her* make a fool out of me? You let her scare your own brother?"

"Didn't scare me!" Joshua blew himself up like a proud dragon again. Then he looked sheepish. "Well, she only scared me a little. Jennifer warned me. That was our secret."

Lisa gasped, even more furious. Jennifer drew her feet up on her chair and hid her face against her knees. Then Jennifer noticed that Lisa was standing up tall, while she *cringed.* Jennifer lifted her head. "I tried to tell you how I felt last night."

"Last night all you did was run away," Lisa answered scornfully.

"Tonight I told you I'd talked to Echo." Jennifer stood up. "You wouldn't listen. You never listen . . . even if you are my friend."

Lisa folded her arms. "I *was* your friend." She deliberately turned away.

Lisa had never said that to her before. The words pierced Jennifer. She couldn't seem to breathe. "Lisa?" her voice cracked.

Her best friend didn't answer.

14. One Last Story

Echo poured three glasses of orange juice. First she handed one to Jennifer, trying to tell her something with her eyes, but Jennifer didn't understand. She put the other two glasses down on the table. Then Echo said calmly, "You children have no right to try to drive me away from my new home. I'm not hurting you. I just want to live my life the way I wish."

Joshua zipped in between Echo and the table to get his juice. "You live *weird*!"

"Joshua!" Jennifer cried, but her voice was little more than a whisper. She was still staring at Lisa.

"Well, she does." Joshua sat down at the kitchen table. Before he took a sip, he said politely, "Thanks for the orange juice."

Echo laughed.

The laughter blew away the frozen panic inside Jennifer about Lisa. Jennifer sat down and drank a swallow of her orange juice. Then she drank half the glass.

She was curious about how Echo lived, too. Echo didn't leave the house every day to work. And she didn't have any kids. Jennifer thought of what Echo had said earlier. "A book?"

"I write children's books," Echo explained.

A writer, Jennifer thought. *Not an actor.* Then Jennifer closed her eyes, trying to remember exactly. "When you turned the light on, you said, 'That scene will be perfect in my book.' " Jennifer gasped. "Does that mean you acted out this whole evening to put in a story? The spell, the pot, even the witch's costume?" Gleefully, she wrapped her sheet tighter around herself. "Are *we* going to be in a book?!"

Echo turned off the burner under her whistling teapot. The teapot whistled on two notes like a harmonica. "Not precisely. *You* won't be in the book." She poured the hot water into her cup and stirred. "But some of what you did might be. Like Lisa swinging on the rope with that wonderful skeleton tied below her. And you, Jennifer, with that plastic hand covered with ketchup, convinced I would believe it was real. And Joshua saying, 'I don't want my toes in a jar!' "

Echo leaned against the counter. "I always try to act out my stories before I write them. That's why I was climbing that tree when I first moved in. My main character in my book climbs a tree, and I hadn't climbed a tree in years." Echo blushed a little, as if she were embarrassed. "Then I saw that cat who had been sneaking into my house and scaring my canary."

"Mr. Davis's cat, Milks," Jennifer explained.

Joshua pointed to the giant steaming pot on the stove. "How . . . how did . . . ?"

Looking at the pot made Jennifer feel nervous, too. "We *saw* that cloth change color."

Echo giggled like a little girl.

"That's an old dyeing trick," Echo said. "A weaver in the National Museum at Wales taught it to me years ago. I thought it might come in handy some day in one of my books. It has something to do with how the air reacts with the dye. Wonderful trick, isn't it?"

Jennifer finished her orange juice. She'd never talked to a writer before. "What about that night on the porch, when you were dressed in the robe? Will you use that in one of your books?"

Echo sat on the countertop while she

poured her tea. "I'm writing a fantasy story about a girl who runs away. She meets this strange woman who sings to the moon."

Lisa stepped closer, interested despite herself. "And the sword fight? Is that in your book?"

Jennifer stiffened. Now Lisa would find out about her exaggerating that story.

"I decided to leave that part out," Echo said simply. Jennifer wanted to hug her.

"How did you keep so many flowers growing in October?" Joshua demanded. "We believed the snapdragons would come alive on Halloween."

Echo grinned, a bit wickedly. "I covered the flowers with all my old sheets during that last frost. Pretty witchy, huh?" She crossed her arms.

Joshua blushed, but that didn't stop him from asking, "What about when you were sitting with those people in a circle. Will that be in your book, too?"

Echo took a deep breath before she spoke. "No! That's not in my book. We were just meditating." Her eyes narrowed. "I have a right to my privacy! Will you children *stop* looking in that window?"

First Joshua nodded, then Jennifer. She meant it, too. She would never *ever* spy on Echo again. Lisa looked away with a fierce expression on her face.

"I'm sorry," Joshua whispered.

Echo said more gently, "That you spied?"

"I'm sorry . . ." his voice could barely be heard, ". . . that I hurt your flowers."

"Me, too," Jennifer whispered. She squeezed her little brother's hand. Maybe he wouldn't grow up to be seven feet tall, skinny, and vicious after all.

Lisa stood with her back to the Catlady, her arms folded. With a sigh, Echo turned to Jennifer and Joshua. "And I'm sorry I scared you tonight. I have such a temper.

I know I should have simply told your parents about the garden, but—"

"Tell Dad?" Joshua exclaimed. "NO!!"

Even Lisa was looking at Echo now.

"Help me re-plant my garden, then," Echo said. "Every day after school. I've got hundreds of bulbs to plant and bushes to prune."

"Every day?" Joshua plunked his juice glass down hard on the table.

"Every day," Echo replied firmly. "If you aren't here right at three . . ." She shrugged.

"You'll turn us into foxes?" Joshua suggested.

Echo waited seriously for their response.

Jennifer realized that she liked the idea of working in Echo's garden. "I'll be there," she said. Making the garden pretty again would help her feel better about the ruined flowers. Besides, this would be her chance to get to know Echo. In a way, it seemed more of a reward than a punishment.

"Me, too," Joshua agreed.

Even Lisa nodded her agreement. She'd better. Jennifer knew that her mother would refuse to let her play sports for the rest of the year if she found out about the garden.

Joshua stood up in his seat. "Tell us a story," he said.

Echo shook her head. Jennifer tugged on her brother's hand. "Sit down," she whispered.

"Pleeeeeease." Joshua begged again. He smiled slyly. "It will make me feel better."

Echo looked at him, her head tilted, as if deciding. Then she said, "We'll all tell a story. *Our* story."

Joshua sat down with a thump. "She *is* weird," he said. Jennifer kicked him under the table.

"How do we start?" Echo asked. The children stared at her. Even Lisa was looking at her again. "How do you start a story?" Echo repeated.

"Once upon a time," Joshua piped up.

"There were three children named Lisa, Jennifer, and Joshua," Jennifer added. She was good at this.

"One day when they were walking to school," Echo said, "they saw their new neighbor climbing a tree."

Echo pointed at Lisa. Lisa bit her lower lip and shook her head. Echo waited.

"That's your new neighbor?" Lisa finally whispered.

Joshua hopped down off his seat and skipped around and around the table. "Crazy. Crazy. Crazy."

Echo pulled a pad out of a kitchen drawer and pushed the paper toward Jennifer. "You write it down." She handed her a red pen.

Jennifer took the pad, astonished. Echo was giving the paper to her? Echo was a real writer, and she wanted *her* to write it down? "Start over!" Jennifer exclaimed.

"Once upon a time," Joshua repeated, still skipping.

Jennifer wrote furiously. After a page and a half, she put down the pen and shook her aching hand. Maybe she should write down some of her own stories from now on. Like Echo. It would sure get her into a lot less trouble. Even Dad would be happier.

What had Echo said to her on that rainy day?

Dream!

Just at that moment, Joshua cried in an anguished voice, "What about trick or treating?"

"Not yet!" Jennifer and Lisa responded. Jennifer was amazed that Lisa would say that . . . that Lisa wanted to stay longer.

Then Jennifer realized that she and Lisa had said the words in unison. Jennifer waited, unable to even move. Then Lisa leaned toward her. They tapped foreheads solemnly . . . just the way they had always done.

Lisa squished her cat tail between her hands. "I'm still angry at you, Jennifer, for not telling me that tonight was pretending." But she didn't look *too* mad.

For the first time that evening, Lisa looked right at Echo without glaring. "Your trick was even better than ours! How did you ever think it up?" Jennifer knew that was Lisa's way of apologizing.

Echo shrugged. "I'm a writer, remember? I like to think things up."

Just like me, Jennifer thought.

Echo went into the other room and came back with her bowl of treats. "Eat all you want."

"Wow!" Joshua opened a Milky Way and a Butterfinger. He took a bite of each. Lisa chose a candy bar of solid chocolate. Jennifer plucked a Hershey's Kiss from the bowl.

"Now, where were we with our story?" Echo asked.

Jennifer licked her fingers. Then she picked up her pen. She had a feeling, a crazy feeling, that she might be doing a lot of writing from now on.

About the Author

Susan Clymer likes animals. She likes to walk in the wilderness and do things that seem impossible. "But most of all," she says, "I love to write."

This is the fifth book that Ms. Clymer has written for young readers. Her other books are *The One and Only Bunbun*, *The Glass Mermaid*, *Four Month Friend*, and *Scrawny, the Classroom Duck.*

When she's not busy writing her own books, Ms. Clymer visits schools, reads to children, and helps them write stories, too.

She has a daughter, Micaya, and lives in Fairway, Kansas.